The Chronicles of Nice Guy Maso

written by
Monyetta Shaw

MYND MATTERS

THE EVAN GRACE GROUP

Books may be purchased in quantity and/or special sales by contacting the publisher.

Mynd Matters Publishing
715 Peachtree Street NE
Suites 100 & 200
Atlanta, GA 30308
www.myndmatterspublishing.com

ISBN: 978-1-953307-27-9 (paperback)
ISBN: 978-1-953307-28-6 (hardcover)

FIRST EDITION

TO MASON & MADILYN,

MY PRECIOUS M'S. YOU TWO ARE
SUPER KIND, SMART, CREATIVE,
AND FEARLESS WITH LIGHTS THAT
ALREADY SHINE SO BRIGHT.

I AM SO BLESSED AND HONORED
TO STAND IN YOUR LIGHT EACH
DAY AND FEEL THE WARMTH OF
YOUR LOVE.

YOU ARE MY JOY...MY
STRENGTH...MY REASONS! I LOVE
YOU BEYOND.

—MOMMY

"GO BE GREAT!" MOMMY SAYS AS SHE DOES EVERY MORNING. I SMILE BACK AT HER AS MY SISTER MADI AND I HOP OUT OF THE CAR FROM CARPOOL.

"TODAY IS GOING TO BE A SUPER DUPER FANTASTIC DAY! I CAN FEEL IT!" I SAY OPTIMISTICALLY.

"MASO, YOU SAY THAT EVERY DAY," MADI SAYS BEFORE DASHING UP TO MEET HER FRIENDS ON THE PLAYGROUND BEFORE CLASS STARTS.

MAYBE I DO SAY IT EVERY DAY BUT IT'S BECAUSE IT'S TRUE. I SMILE THINKING OF THE ENDLESS POSSIBILITIES.

"HEY GUYS!" I SAY AS I WALK TOWARDS MY FRIENDS JACK, DECLAN, AND MILLIE, WHO ALMOST ALWAYS MEET ME AT THE STEPS.

"COOL SHOES," COMMENTS JACK AS HE LOOKS DOWN AT MY FEET. I NOD AND TELL HIM THANKS AS OUR LITTLE GROUP HEADS THROUGH THE DOORS OF THE SCHOOL.

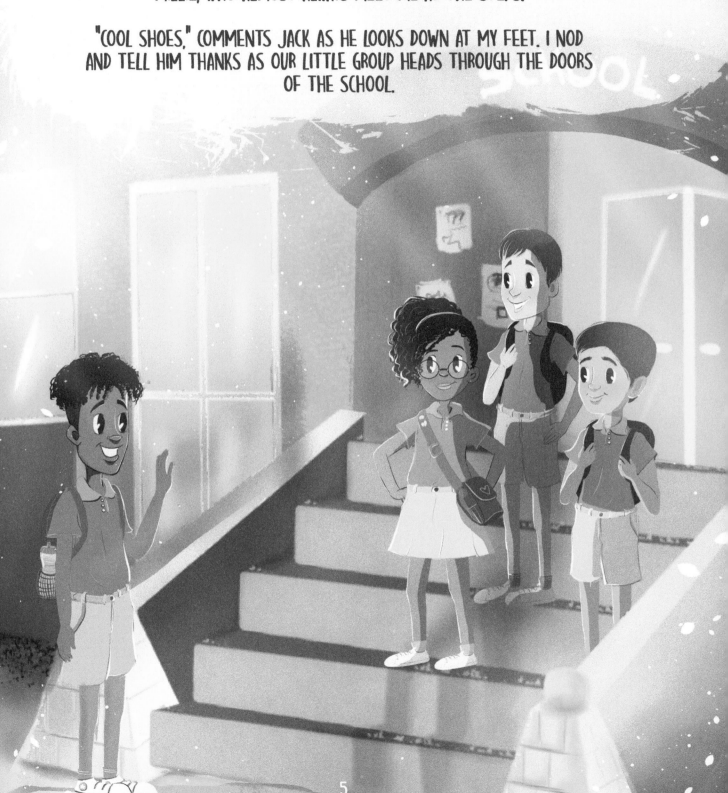

I STOP BY THE LIBRARY TO RETURN A FEW BOOKS.

"GREAT READS, MASON," SAYS MR. BUCKLES. "WHAT ARE YOU READING NEXT?
SOMETHING ABOUT MYSTERIES AND SUPER HEROES?"

"GOOD MORNING, MASON," SAYS THE MUSIC TEACHER, MRS. G, WITH A SMILE. "GREAT JOB IN SATURDAY'S SOCCER GAME."

"YEAH, WAY TO TURN IT AROUND BUDDY!" SAYS MR. CLAY FROM THE OTHER SIDE OF THE ROOM.

"THANK YOU MUCH," I SAY WITH PRIDE. I AM GETTING PRETTY GOOD AFTER ALL.

AS WE MAKE OUR WAY TO THE CLASSROOM, I NOTICE SOMETHING DIFFERENT ABOUT MY TEACHER, MRS. FOUTS. "I LIKE YOUR HAIRCUT, MRS. FOUTS."

HER FACE LIGHTS UP AS SHE TOUCHES HER HAIR.

"THANK YOU VERY MUCH FOR NOTICING, MASON."

I PUT MY BACKPACK AND WATER BOTTLE AWAY AND RUSH TO MY DESK TO START MY JOURNAL. I CANNOT WAIT TO WRITE ABOUT MY SOCCER GAME AND THE FUN WEEKEND WITH MY FAMILY.

JUST AS I'M GETTING INTO THE DETAILS, MRS. FOUTS ASKS THE CLASS TO GIVE HER OUR UNDIVIDED ATTENTION.

"CLASS, THIS IS OUR NEW STUDENT, FELIPE, PLEASE WELCOME HIM TO OUR CLASSROOM."

I SMILE AND WAVE AT FELIPE BECAUSE I LOVE MEETING NEW FRIENDS. A FEW KIDS SNICKER FROM ACROSS THE ROOM. I DO NOT LIKE IT AT ALL. WHAT IF SOMEONE DID THAT TO THEM. LAUGHING AT SOMEONE DOESN'T MAKE THEM FEEL GOOD OR WELCOME.

I LATER VOLUNTEER TO SHOW FELIPE AROUND THE CLASSROOM. I EXPLAIN SOME OF THE COOL THINGS ABOUT OUR CLASS AND WE DISCUSS WHERE HE'S FROM AND HIS OLD SCHOOL. I FIND OUT HIS FAMILY HAD TO MOVE BECAUSE HIS DAD'S JOB RELOCATED HERE.

BEFORE LONG, IT IS LUNCHTIME. AS I GO TO TAKE MY USUAL SEAT AT THE TABLE WITH MY FRIENDS, I NOTICE FELIPE SITTING AT THE VERY END OF A DIFFERENT TABLE, LOOKING SAD. I WONDER WHY BUT THEN I OVERHEAR SOME OF MY CLASSMATES MAKING FUN OF HIM AND LAUGHING.

"HOW COULD HE EVER THINK HE COULD SIT WITH US?" SAYS JULIEN, LOUDLY.

"I KNOW! HE'S DENITELY NOT COOL ENOUGH TO EAT LUNCH WITH US," SAYS VICKI, ANOTHER ONE OF MY CLASSMATES, AS EVERYONE ELSE LAUGHS.

I SHAKE MY HEAD AND WALK RIGHT ON OVER AND TELL THEM EXACTLY HOW I FEEL ABOUT THEIR COMMENTS.

"HEY, THAT'S NOT NICE! HOW WOULD YOU FEEL IF SOMEONE TREATED YOU THAT WAY? WHY DON'T YOU TRY TO GET TO KNOW FELIPE INSTEAD OF MAKING FUN OF HIM? HE'S ACTUALLY VERY NICE."

I SMILE PROUDLY HOPING THEY'LL SEE THINGS MY WAY. INSTEAD, A STRANGE THING HAPPENS. THEY START MOCKING ME!

"YOU ALWAYS HAVE TO BE THE NICE GUY, DON'T YOU?" ASKS ONE OF MY CLASSMATES SARCASTICALLY.

THEN JULIEN ASKS, "DO YOU THINK YOU'RE GOING TO WIN AN AWARD FOR BEING A NICE GUY OR SOMETHING?"

BEFORE I KNOW IT, THEY ALL START LAUGHING AND CHANTING, "NICE GUY MASO! NICE GUY MASO!" OVER AND OVER AGAIN.

I FEEL A LITTLE EMBARRASSED AND LOOK AROUND TO SEE IF ANYONE IS WATCHING. THEN, IT HITS ME. BEING CALLED A NICE GUY, EVEN IF THEY ARE SAYING IT TO HURT ME, IS A GOOD THING!

I SMILE BROADLY AND THINK, I AM NICE GUY MASO!

I WALK OVER TO FELIPE AND ASK IF I CAN JOIN HIM FOR LUNCH.

"OF COURSE, MASON!" HE RESPONDS EXCITEDLY.

AS WE EAT OUR LUNCHES, HE LOOKS UP AND ASKS WHY I DECIDED TO SIT WITH HIM.
I REPLY, "WHY NOT!"

HIS SMILE WIDENS AND HE SITS UP A LITTLE TALLER. I FEEL GREAT INSIDE BECAUSE
I KNOW I DID THE RIGHT THING.

WHEN I GET HOME, I CAN'T WAIT TO TELL MY PARENTS ALL ABOUT THE NEW STUDENT AND WHAT HAPPENED. MOM SAYS SHE IS SUPER PROUD OF ME FOR STEPPING UP! SHE ALSO ADDS THAT NO ONE SHOULD EVER JUDGE A PERSON BY THE WAY THEY LOOK. THE COLOR OF THEIR SKIN, THEIR GENDER, OR THEIR RELIGION SHOULD NOT MATTER EITHER. WE SHOULD ACCEPT PEOPLE FOR WHO THEY ARE AND FOCUS ON THEIR CHARACTER AND HOW THEY TREAT OTHERS.

IT IS SO COOL TO BE KIND TO OTHERS! A SMILE AND A SIMPLE HELLO CAN CHANGE A PERSON'S DAY. SHE ALWAYS SAYS THAT.

"MOM, YOU ARE SO RIGHT BECAUSE I FELT REALLY GOOD TAKING UP FOR FELIPE AND HE LOOKED HAPPY AFTERWARDS."

I CALL MY DAD RIGHT AFTER OUR TALK TO TELL HIM ABOUT MY DAY. HE IS ALSO PROUD OF ME.

"NICE GUY MASO HAS A GOOD RING TO IT," HE SAYS.

"I THINK SO TOO. CAN YOU CALL ME NICE GUY MASO FROM NOW ON?"

HE LAUGHS AND RESPONDS, "SURE THING, KIDDO."

HE ALWAYS TELLS ME LIONS DON'T TURN WHEN DOGS ARE BARKING. ALTHOUGH I DIDN'T QUITE UNDERSTAND WHAT HE MEANT BEFORE, I DO NOW. SOMETIMES BULLIES SHOULD BE IGNORED BUT THIS TIME IT'S DIFFERENT. I'M NOT AFRAID TO STAND UP TO THE BULLIES IN MY CLASS AND DO THE RIGHT THING.

THE NEXT MORNING, AFTER MOM DROPS US OFF, I RUSH TO THE PLAYGROUND BEFORE SCHOOL STARTS. MOST OF MY FRIENDS ARE ALREADY THERE PLAYING.

ALL BUT FELIPE.

I SEE HIM STANDING ALONE ON THE OPPOSITE END OF THE PLAYGROUND AND WALK OVER TO SEE IF HE IS OKAY.

A FEW OF THE KIDS STOP PLAYING AND WALK OVER TO US SINGING THE SAME CHANT FROM THE DAY BEFORE.

"NICE GUY MASO! NICE GUY MASO!"

"THANKS! I LOVE MY NEW NICKNAME BECAUSE IT IS SUPER COOL TO BE KIND. YOU GUYS SHOULD TRY IT."

I REMEMBER WHAT MY MOM TOLD ME AND SHARE IT WITH THEM.

"WE SHOULD ALL TAKE THE TIME TO GET TO KNOW A PERSON AND NOT JUDGE SOMEONE BY WHAT THEY LOOK LIKE. JUDGE PEOPLE BY THEIR CHARACTER AND GIVE EVERYONE A CHANCE. FELIPE IS NEW HERE AND WE SHOULD GET TO KNOW HIM AND MAKE HIM FEEL WELCOME."

"YOU'RE RIGHT MASO," SAYS TWO OF THE GUYS IN UNISON.

"FELIPE, WE APOLOGIZE FOR NOT BEING NICE TO YOU YESTERDAY," SAYS JULIEN.

THE REST OF THE KIDS APOLOGIZE TO FELIPE AND JULIEN ASKS IF HE'D LIKE TO PLAY WITH THEM AT RECESS AFTER LUNCH.

"YES, THAT'D BE GREAT!" SAYS FELIPE JUST AS THE SCHOOL BELL RINGS.

EVERYONE RUSHES TO GRAB THEIR BACKPACKS AND WE ALL HEAD INSIDE.

LATER THAT DAY

EVERYONE GOT ALONG DURING RECESS AND FELIPE SEEMED MORE RELAXED AROUND OUR CLASSMATES.

AS WE HEAD BACK INSIDE, I FOLLOW CLOSE BEHIND BUT HAVE TO STOP TO TIE MY SHOE.

"DO YOU WANT ME TO WAIT ON YOU MASO?" ASKS FELIPE AS HE TURNS IN MY DIRECTION.

"NO, IT'S OKAY. I'LL MEET YOU INSIDE," I TELL HIM.

JUST AS I START TO STAND UP, I NOTICE A BRIGHT, COLORFUL LIGHT GLOWING FROM A SMALL CRACK IN THE NEARBY BRICK WALL.

I SLOWLY WALK OVER TO SEE WHAT IT COULD BE. I LEAN IN CLOSER, STILL NOT SURE, AND AFTER A FEW SECONDS, I REACH DOWN TO CAREFULLY DISLODGE IT FROM THE WALL. ONCE IN HAND, I WIPE IT OFF AND LOOK AT IT CLOSELY.

IT IS A RARE QUARTZ CRYSTAL.

"WOW! IT IS SO BEAUTIFUL," I SAY SLIGHTLY UNDER MY BREATH. I IMMEDIATELY FEEL ENTRANCED BY THE RARE STONE.

THE LONGER I HOLD IT, THE MORE I BEGIN TO FEEL DIFFERENT. THINGS BECOME HAZY AS I BLINK SEVERAL TIMES IN AN ATTEMPT TO FOCUS MY EYES.

WHEN I TURN TO WALK TOWARDS THE SCHOOL, THE CRYSTAL ILLUMINATES SO BRIGHTLY, IT LIGHTS UP THE ENTIRE SKY.

I STOP WALKING BECAUSE I CAN'T LIFT MY FEET. THEY FEEL HEAVY LIKE LEAD.
I LOOK UP AND MY EYES WIDEN AT WHAT I SEE. I STAND, STARING WITH DISBELIEF.

SUDDENLY, A FORCE HITS ME AND EVERYTHING GOES DARK FOR SEVERAL SECONDS...

WONDERING WHAT HAPPENS NEXT?
STAY TUNED FOR MASON'S NEW MYSTERY!